WINNIE-THE-POOH AND TIGGER TOO

Rabbit was a very sociable sort of person with lots of friends and relations. There were just two things that Rabbit didn't like. One was a visit from Pooh when he was looking for a Little Something, and the other was being bounced by Tigger. So Rabbit thought up a plan. . .and that was how Pooh and Tigger got lost in the Forest.

Other titles in this series:

POOH AND THE HONEY TREE
POOH AND PIGLET GO HUNTING
WINNIE-THE-POOH AND THE BLUSTERY DAY
POOH IN A TIGHT PLACE

Scholastic Book Services Inc.,
10 Earlham Street, London WC2H 9LN

Scholastic Inc.,
730 Broadway, New York, NY 10003, USA

Scholastic Tab Publications Ltd.,
123 Newkirk Road, Richmond Hill,
Ontario L4C 3G5, Canada

Ashton Scholastic Pty Ltd., Box 579, Gosford,
New South Wales, Australia

Ashton Scholastic Ltd., 165 Marua Road,
Panmure, Auckland, New Zealand

First published in West Germany by Ravensburger Taschenbücher, 1983
First published in the UK by Scholastic Book Services Inc. 1985
Illustrations copyright © Walt Disney, 1983
This translation copyright © Scholastic Book Services Inc. 1985
Translated by Anthea Bell
Original title *Die Geschichten vom Tiger*
ISBN 0 590 70411 7

Made and printed in Spain by
Printer industria gráfica s.a. Barcelona
D.L.B. 2932-1985

WINNIE-THE-POOH AND TIGGER TOO

Translated by Anthea Bell

Hippo Books
Scholastic Book Services
London

My Best Friend Pooh

I've known Pooh Bear for years and years. I should think I've known him for more than fifty years!

My name is Christopher Robin, and we used to share a room. I mean, Pooh and my other friends lived with me. Grown-ups said they were just stuffed toys, but I know better!

There were Pooh and Piglet, Rabbit and his relations, and then there was bouncy Tigger. We lived in a wonderful place called Hundred Acre Wood, in the middle of the Forest, and of course the Forest and the Wood were real.

"Hallo, Pooh Bear!"

"Hallo, Christopher Robin!" said Pooh. "Are you going to tell another story?"

Winnie-the-Pooh lived in the Forest too, of course.

Pooh was fond of making up Songs and Hums. He wrote most of the poetry that was written in the Forest, and he could make up a song for almost any occasion.

He used to sing a song about himself, which went:

"Winnie-the-Pooh, Winnie-the-Pooh!
Tubby little cubby all stuffed with fluff!
I'm Winnie-the-Pooh, Winnie-the-Pooh!
Willy-nilly silly old Bear!"

But the songs he liked best were all about honey.

"Isn't it funny
How a bear likes honey?
Buzz! Buzz! Buzz!
I wonder why he does?"

Pooh Bear was very fond of honey indeed.

He had eaten so much honey he was getting quite fat, and he did his Stoutness Exercises every day when he got up. That was about eleven o'clock, so it was time for elevenses as well. TIM FOUR A LITEL SUMHTING, Pooh called it.

There was something Pooh was trying to remember today. But as he was a Bear of Very Little Brain, he found it difficult. "Think, think, think," he told himself. "What *did* I want to think of?"

And while Winnie-the-Pooh was thinking. . .

Tigger

. . .the door burst open, and in bounced Tigger. He bounced at Pooh.

"Hallooo!" said Tigger.

"My goodness me!" said Pooh. "You frightened me!"

"Of course I did!" said Tigger. "I'm very frightening! Who are *you?*"

"I'm Pooh," said Pooh.

"What's a Pooh?"

"You're sitting on one."

"Oh, I see. I'm Tigger," said Tigger. "T - I - G - G - E - R."

"What's a Tigger?" asked Pooh.

"You ask a lot of questions!" said Tigger, but he got off Pooh at last.

Suddenly Tigger saw a very strange animal in
Pooh's looking-glass. He was frightened of it.
"What's that funny animal?" he asked. "Look at
its funny eyes and mouth and its silly
stripes. . ." And he closed his own eyes.
"Has it gone away yet, Pooh?" he asked,
sounding scared.

Poor Tigger had been really frightened. Pooh
Bear tried to make him feel better. He even gave
him some honey to eat, because honey is
soothing and good for the nerves. Or so Pooh
thought, and it was not easy for him to give any
of his honey away. But it turned out that Tiggers
don't like honey.

However, he soon got over his fright, once he realized that the strange animal was only his own reflection. And next minute. . .

. . .he was bouncing at Pooh again. "Hallooo! I'm Tigger!" he shouted. "T - I - G - G - "

"I know," said Pooh, crossly. "This is the second time you've bounced me, and after I gave you some honey, too! I don't call that friendly!"

"Oh, I'm always bouncy!" said Tigger. "That's my own way of being friendly!"

"Do you always sit on your friends?" asked Pooh.

"Yes," said Tigger. "It's nice and comfortable, don't you think?"

Pooh didn't.

Luckily Tigger soon went away. "Got to bounce at a few more people!" he said.

Watching him go, Pooh thought Tiggers were rather tiring animals.

But that was Tigger all over. He always bounced at his friends when they were least expecting it.

He went to see Piglet next. Piglet, being a very small animal, didn't like being bounced at in the least.

He sat down rather suddenly. "What did you have to go and do that for, Tigger?" he asked.

"Oh, that was only a little bounce!" said Tigger,

cheerfully.

"I suppose you'll be telling me I was lucky next," said Piglet.

"So you were!" said Tigger. "I'm keeping my big bounces for Rabbit!"

And off he went.

Long Ears

Long Ears was Tigger's name for Rabbit. I don't think you've met Rabbit yet. Rabbit was a very sociable sort of person, with lots of friends and relations, but he hadn't been seen much lately. He had been busy working in his garden and harvesting his carrots. He had grown lots of carrots to last him all winter. Carrots were what he liked to eat best of all.

He had plenty of other things in his larder too. He had honey, and condensed milk. But there were two things Rabbits don't like. One was a visit from Pooh, because Pooh ate so much of his condensed milk and honey, and the other was being bounced by Tigger.

And what Tigger liked best of all was bouncing at Rabbit.

"Hi, Rabbit!" shouted Tigger. "I'm Tigger! T - I - G - "

"Don't bother to spell it!" said Rabbit crossly. "Tigger, you're terrible! Just look at my garden!"

"Messy, isn't it, Long Ears?" said Tigger.

"*Messy?*" Rabbit was losing his temper. And when Rabbit lost his temper, he lost it very badly! "Messy?" he said. "You've ruined my garden! Why don't you ever stop bouncing?"

"Because bouncing is what Tiggers do best!" said Tigger, and he sang Rabbit his song.

"The wonderful thing about Tiggers,
Is Tiggers are wonderful things!
Their tops are made out of rubber.
Their bottoms are made out of springs.
They're bouncy, trouncy, founcy, bouncy,
Fun, fun, fun, fun, fun!
But the most wonderful thing about Tiggers,
Is I'm the only one!"

The Meeting

Rabbit was getting tired of Tigger being so bouncy. He thought up a plan to unbounce him. Yes, he was sure that would be a good idea! But he wasn't sure just *how* to unbounce a Tigger. So he called a meeting of himself, Pooh and Piglet.

Rabbit made a little speech, as people do at meetings. "My friends," said Rabbit, "I'm glad to see so many of you at this meeting. We are holding it to discuss Tigger. Tigger is getting on our nerves. We ought to teach him a lesson. It's high time to unbounce him. We. . ."

Piglet interrupted. "That would be a good idea if we could think of a *way* to unbounce him, Rabbit," he said.

"Exactly," said Rabbit. "What do *you* think, Pooh?"

But Pooh, who was feeling sleepy, hadn't been listening. It was three o'clock in the afternoon, and Pooh always felt sleepy at three o'clock in the afternoon, as Rabbit should have remembered. And anyway Pooh thought

speeches were boring. They sent him to sleep.
"What do *you* think?" Rabbit repeated.
Pooh woke up all of a sudden and said,
"Extremely!"
"Extremely what?"
"Whatever you were saying. Undoubtedly!"

"Pooh," said Piglet, "didn't you hear what Rabbit asked you?"

"Of course I did," said Pooh. "But I think I've got a bit of fluff in one ear. Could you ask your question again, Rabbit?"

"Which bit of it, Pooh?"

"From whenever I got the fluff in my ear," said Pooh.

"When was that?" asked Rabbit, impatiently.

"I don't know," said Pooh, yawning. "I couldn't hear it all."

"We were wondering," said Rabbit, "how to unbounce Tigger."

Then Rabbit suddenly had an idea. "I know what we'll do!" he said. "Listen: we'll take Tigger on a long expedition!"

"What's an Expotition?" asked Piglet.

"A long explore," said Rabbit. "We'll take him out on a walk somewhere he's never been, and then we'll lose him. We can come and find him again next morning of course, and you mark my words, he'll be a gentle Tigger by then, a humble Tigger, a small and sorry Tigger! It will teach

him a lesson, and he'll never bounce at us again. Who agrees with my plan?"

"I do," said Piglet, and he gave Pooh a nudge. "Wake up, Pooh!"

Pooh jumped. "I do –" he began.

"Good!" said Rabbit. "Motion unanimously carried!"

He was already looking forward to putting his plan into practice.

Pooh and Piglet in the Forest

They set off next morning. It was a cold and misty day, and Pooh had forgotten to bring anything to eat! As you know, Pooh was a Bear of Very Little Brain. Tigger went on ahead of the others, and kept bouncing into the mist. Suddenly they lost sight of him. Rabbit decided this was the time to lose Tigger.

"This is our moment!" he said. "Quick, hide!"

"Is Tigger lost now?" asked Piglet, rather worried.

"Yes, and he'll come looking for us, but he won't find us," said Rabbit happily. "That was our plan, wasn't it, Pooh?"

"Well, yes," said Pooh. "But I feel a bit sorry for Tigger."

"Never mind Tigger! My plan's worked!" Rabbit boasted.

"Yes, but. . ." said Pooh. "I mean, it's lunchtime! My tummy's grumbling. Can't you hear it?"

The others couldn't – but they heard a voice instead. "Hallooo!" It was Tigger! Rabbit was very cross.

"Quick, hide in that hollow tree!" he said.

"Hallooo there, Pooh, Piglet, Rabbit!" said Tigger. "Oh – they must have gone off somewhere! Hallooo! Where are you all?" Tigger couldn't see the others anywhere. He was beginning to feel worried about them.

"We're here, of course!" growled Pooh.
"Ssh! Keep quiet!" said Rabbit crossly, but he
said it in a whisper. Piglet's heart was thumping
rather hard.

"I *am* keeping quiet!" growled Pooh, feeling hurt.

"Well, that's funny," said Tigger. "I say, where are you? Say something! Rabbit! Pooh! Piglet! Where are you?"

Tigger was feeling very puzzled now. Pooh just managed to stop himself answering again. He was a Helpful Bear, and was usually glad to answer questions if he could. But Rabbit glared at him, so he kept his mouth shut.

Tigger's tail got stuck in a crack in the trunk of

the hollow tree – and pulling it out, he very
nearly found the three other animals. But he
didn't see them. He went bouncing away
through the misty Forest, looking for his friends.

"There!" said Rabbit pleased. "That's got rid of
him! Come on, hurry up, you two! Let's go
home!"
Rabbit was sure Tigger must be lost by now. But

suddenly he stopped. "I think we've been past this place before!" he said in surprise.

"You're right, Rabbit," said Pooh. "We *have* been past this sandpit before."

Rabbit marched on through the mist. "It's a lucky thing I know the Forest so well!" he told the other two. "If I didn't, we might get lost. You'd better follow me."

After a while Pooh began to get tired of seeing the same sandpit over and over again. They had now passed it five times. Whichever way they went, they still came back to it. Pooh drew an arrow in the sand, but it didn't help much, because he drew it like this:

Pooh Bear was thinking hard, and suddenly he had a good idea.

"Rabbit, I've had a good idea!" said Pooh. "Why don't we walk away from this pit and then *try* to

find it again?"

"What for?" asked Piglet, puzzled.

"Because we keep looking for the way home, and finding the sandpit again," said Pooh. "So I thought if we look for the sandpit, we'll find the way home instead."

"I don't see any sense in that!" snapped Rabbit. "Now, if I walked away from this sandpit and then looked for it, of course I'd find it again. I'll show you! You two wait here!"

And Rabbit walked off into the mist alone.

Pooh's Tummy Rumbles

Pooh and Piglet stood in the mist, waiting for Rabbit.
They waited and they waited.

And Pooh had plenty of time to think of all the pots of honey in his cupboard at home.

"Pooh, what was that funny noise?" asked Piglet, sounding scared.

"My tummy, rumbling," said Pooh. "Come on, let's go home!"

"Oh, Pooh!" said Piglet. "Do you know the way?"

"No, Piglet, but there are twelve pots of honey in my cupboard," said Pooh, who felt sure Christopher Robin would have made sure they were all full for him. "And those twelve pots of honey called to my tummy just now, and my tummy answered them."

"Are you sure, Pooh?" asked Piglet, doubtfully.

"Yes, Piglet. The only reason I couldn't hear them before was because Rabbit *would* keep talking. But I know where they called from. We've only got to follow my tummy."

So they set off. Pooh could hear his pots of honey calling loud and clear. Piglet kept very quiet, so as not to interrupt them.

And when the mist slowly began to lift, even Piglet could see where they were. . .

"Hallooo, you two! Where have *you* been?" asked Tigger. He had been looking for his friends everywhere, and now at last he had found two of them.

"Oh, just looking for the way home," said Pooh.

"Pooh, I don't think Rabbit's plan has worked," whispered Piglet, sounding worried.

"Where is Rabbit, anyway?" asked Tigger.

"He must be lost in the mist," said Pooh.

"Don't you worry!" said Tigger. "*I'll* find him! See you soon! I'll be back in a moment with Rabbit!" And Tigger bounced away.

Sure enough, Rabbit *had* got lost in the mist. It kept playing tricks on him. He didn't like it at all. In fact, Rabbit was beginning to feel a very small and sorry Rabbit indeed.

But luckily Tigger soon found him.

"Tigger!" said Rabbit. "But you're supposed to be lost!"

"Tiggers *never* get lost!" said Tigger.

"What, *never*?" said Rabbit. "Are you *sure*?"

"Come on, Rabbit, let's go home! Off we go!" said Tigger, bouncing away again. He bounced like anything, all the way back, and Rabbit trotted meekly along behind him.

Rabbit and Tigger were soon friends again, of course. Nobody can be quarrelsome for long in the Forest.

Although of course the animals do have little

quarrels now and then.

Eeyore, the old grey donkey, spoilt Rabbit's plan by telling Christopher Robin about it. So Rabbit was cross with Eeyore. But they soon made up their quarrel again.

Pooh had gone straight to his pots of honey – and
sure enough, they were full.

"Oh, Christopher Robin, you *are* kind!" growled
Pooh Bear happily. "You know how much I like
honey!"

So that is the end of this book about Tigger, Rabbit and of course Winnie-the-Pooh.

"And me!" squeaked Piglet.

Yes, of course. And in the next book you can meet some more of our friends, and I'll tell you more stories about Pooh Bear.

Just in case you've forgotten, I'm Christopher Robin.

When I lived in the Hundred Acre Wood with Pooh and the others I was seven, and grown-ups used to say we made it all up, but that's not true. My stories are all true, as sure as there's a Hundred Acre Wood in the Forest!

The next book has more stories about Pooh, and you will find out if Tiggers can climb trees.

Pooh and Piglet get lost again and find the tracks of a Woozle.

And you will meet some more of my friends – Kanga and Baby Roo.